BIG-LEG MUSIC

ALSO BY DAVID KIRBY

POETRY
THE OPERA LOVER
SARAH BERNHARDT'S LEG
SAVING THE YOUNG MEN OF VIENNA

LITERARY CRITICISM
INDIVIDUAL AND COMMUNITY: VARIATION ON A THEME
IN AMERICAN FICTION *(WITH KENNETH H. BALDWIN)*
AMERICAN FICTION TO 1900: A GUIDE TO INFORMATION SOURCES
GRACE KING
AMERICA'S HIVE OF MONEY: FOREIGN SOURCES
OF AMERICAN FICTION THROUGH HENRY JAMES
THE SUN RISES IN THE EVENING:
MONISM AND QUIETISM IN WESTERN CULTURE
THE PLURAL WORLD: AN INTERDISCIPLINARY GLOSSARY
OF CONTEMPORARY AMERICAN THOUGHT
MARK STRAND AND THE POET'S PLACE IN CONTEMPORARY CULTURE
THE PORTRAIT OF A LADY AND THE TURN OF THE SCREW:
HENRY JAMES AND MELODRAMA
BOYISHNESS IN AMERICAN CULTURE
HERMAN MELVILLE

TEXTBOOK
WRITING POETRY:
WHERE POEMS COME FROM AND HOW TO WRITE THEM

FOR CHILDREN
THE COWS ARE GOING TO PARIS *(WITH ALLEN WOODMAN)*
THE BEAR WHO CAME TO STAY *(WITH ALLEN WOODMAN)*

BIG-LEG MUSIC

DAVID KIRBY

ORCHISES
WASHINGTON
1995

Library of Congress Cataloguing in Publication Data
Kirby, David K.
  Big-leg music / David Kirby.
    p. cm.
  ISBN 0-914061-48-8
  I. Title.
PS3561.I66854 1995
811'.54—dc20   94-42449
                                          CIP

ACKNOWLEDGEMENTS

Versions of the following poems appeared for the first time in these magazines: *Bluff City:* "El Libro de Buen Amor" *Chattahoochee Review:* "The Gigolo in the Gazebo" and "A Poor Unhappy Wretched Sick Miserable Little French Boy" *Coal City Review:* "Your Momma Says Omnia Vincit Amor" *Chelsea:* "The Museum of Desire" and "Virginia Rilke" *Clockwatch Review:* "The Physics of Heaven" and "The Physics of Hell" *Fine Madness:* "Bottomless Cup" and "Let's Get Lost" *The Gettysburg Review:* "Eine Götterdämmerung in Mudville" and "Nosebleed, Gold Digger, KGB, Henry James, Handshake" *The Kenyon Review:* "The Summer of the Cuban Missile Crisis" *Negative Capability:* "Broken Promises" *Ploughshares:* "Lurch, Whose Story Doesn't End" *The Quarterly:* "Persons of Low Affect," "The Talking Cure of Frau Emmy von N.," and "Thinking About What You Wanted Her to Say" *Slipstream:* "The Birth and Untimely Death of the Musical Legacy of the Outlaw Jesse James" *Sonora Review:* "The Flesh Eaters" *Southern Poetry Review:* "White" *The Southern Review:* "Krafft-Ebing's *Aberrations of Sexual Pathology*," "La Forza del Destino in the Tri-State Area," "The Money Changer," "Ode to Languor," and "The Potato Mash (More Indefinite and More Soluble)" *Sun Dog: The Southeast Review:* "Your Famous Story"

Manufactured in the United States of America

Published by Orchises Press
P. O. Box 20602
Alexandria
Virginia
22320-1602

G6E4C2A

to those who made the music
to those the music made

TABLE OF CONTENTS

I

II

III

IV

I

Sam Cooke . . . checked into a Los Angeles motel with a young woman named Elisa Boyer. They registered, though Cooke was married to someone else, as Mr. and Mrs. Sam Cooke, and went into a motel room where, Boyer would later testify, Cooke began to rip her clothes off. She escaped, carrying most of his clothes with her, and fled to call the police from a telephone booth. Cooke, dressed in a sport coat and shoes, chased her and began pounding at the motel manager's door, eventually breaking in on the 55-year-old manager, Bertha Franklin. She shot him three times with a .22 revolver, and when he kept coming at her, took up a heavy walking stick and began clubbing him. He was dead when the police arrived.

—Rock of Ages: The Rolling Stone History of Rock and Roll

Let's Get Lost

In Honolulu I am watching a movie called *Let's Get Lost*.
First I have a question for Hawai'i, though:
how could you possibly be a state? For you are not Kansas
    or even Missouri, even though your money is the same

    as theirs and so are the stamps. While we wait
  for the answer to that one, let's get back to the movie.
Let's Get Lost is about a handsome jazz trumpeter
    named Chet Baker who got hooked on heroin and

    had his teeth knocked out and made a big comeback
  years later, though by then he was toothless
and his face was as lined as the mountains
    overlooking the leeward shore of Oahu.

    In Hawai'i you are either a haole, that is, "ghost"
  or white person, or a local. Or a hapa-haole,
which means mixed breed. I call myself hapa-haole
    because half of me is a ghost, yet the other is, not local blood,

    but nothing, because I'm still working on that other half—
  I haven't lost it yet because I've never really found it.
This is what you do when you're not a great jazz trumpeter:
    try to get what you don't have and not let other people know

    what you're doing. Meanwhile, here's Hawai'i's answer
  to my question: I'm a state because everybody says so.
That makes sense: you are whatever a lot of people say you are,
    which is why people are happiest in crowds,

    in shopping malls, say, or sports stadiums.
  Otherwise, you're outnumbered, with your haole half over-
        shadowed
by the nothing half, which potentially includes Everything.
    Chet Baker was mean to everyone: he alienated his lovers,

and his three grown children sound angry and worthless.
 They were the ones who seem lost: what Chet Baker had done
was lose those parts of himself that he didn't need—
 everybody around him needed them, but he didn't.

 Nietzsche: "When virtue has slept, she will get up more
  refreshed."
 In Chet Baker's case, virtue never woke up at all,
whereas in the rest of us it never really sleeps;
 it tosses and turns and makes itself miserable and us, too.

 Hawai'i, I salute you. You're some place to visit,
 and I would get lost in you if I had the money.
As the lights come up, part of me says do the right thing.
 But the other part says, if you get lost, stay lost.

Broken Promises

I have met them in dark alleys, limping and one-armed;
I have seem them playing cards under a single light-bulb
and tried to join in, but they refused me rudely,
knowing I would only let them win.
I have seen them in the foyers of theaters,
coming back late from the interval
long after the others have taken their seats,
and in deserted shopping malls late at night,
peering at things they can never buy,
and I have found them wandering
in a wood where I too have wandered.

This morning I caught one;
small and stupid, too slow to get away,
it was only a promise I had made to myself once
and then forgot, but it screamed and kicked at me
and ran to join the others, who looked at me with reproach
in their long, sad faces.
When I drew near them, they scurried away,
even though they will sleep in my yard tonight.
I hate them for their ingratitude,
I who have kept countless promises,
as dead now as Shakespeare's children.
"You bastards," I scream,
"you have to love me—I gave you life!"

Thinking About What You Wanted Her to Say

You think about the times
you had to say to someone
I don't love you anymore
and even as you said it
you wanted to say
I take it back
it's not true
not because it wasn't
but because it caused
such pain that you thought
one or both of you would die

or the time that old song,
the good one,
came on the kitchen radio
as you were making supper
and you vowed
to learn the words this time
but when it was over
you were no closer
to knowing them
than you were
when you were seventeen,
in your car,
down by the lake,

saying please,
I don't deserve this,
take it back,
and you could tell
that she wanted to
but you both knew
that if she had
the words would have killed her

and by then
you were a dead man anyway
and so handsome.

Your Momma Says Omnia Vincit Amor

Running down the Via degli Annibaldi
I hear Aretha say
my momma said leave you alone
and as I hurry up the steps
of the church of San Pietro in Vincoli
I hear her say my daddy said come on home
and as I turn to go down the right aisle
she says my doctor said take it easy
and then I stop right in front
of Michelangelo's *Moses:*
oh but your loving is much too strong
for these chain chain chains
which were used to bind St. Peter in Palestine
and are themselves preserved under glass
in the same church. Moses is angry;
he's just seen the Israelites
dancing around the Golden Calf
and now he twists his beard with his right hand
and shifts his weight to the ball of his left foot
so he can jump up and smash the stone tablets
with the Ten Commandments on them.

I'd like to be that angry just once—
or, like Bernini's St. Teresa,
to pass out from pleasure! I think of Bo Diddley
as I scurry down the Via XX Settembre
and up the steps of the church of Santa Maria della Vittoria
with its great Baroque sculpture
in which the angel smiles at the saint
as sweetly as a child would, yet his copper arrow
is aimed between her legs;
God might as well have told Teresa
he walked forty-seven miles of barbed wire,
got a cobra snake for a necktie

and a house by the roadside made out of rattlesnake hide
because, really, the only question is,
Who do you love?

White

I am the whitest person I know,
even though my name is Kirby,
not White, which is the name
of millions of Anglophones,
not to mention
all the Weisses, LeBlancs,
and LoBiancos, each of them
as different as can be
yet all bearing this deceptive name
with its calm surface and
its secret allegiance to itself.

For instance, everyone loves
white bread, certainly when
they are young, yet by the time
they have come to prefer wheat,
rye, or pumpernickel, an educated
few, at least, have learned
to love the White Whale, who
stands for everything, including
a number of things that are
quite terrible; Melville himself
said so. From an electromagnetic
standpoint, white is not one

but all colors, even though
we cannot see them any more
than we can see the white
and dimpled buttocks of the nuns
who work in the garden,
their hands as dark and wrinkled
as the earth itself, the skin
beneath their habits as pale
and smooth as that of the Baby

they will meet some day,
the day of the death of
their whiteness, the birth
of all whiteness everywhere.

Beginning with a Line by E. M. Forster

A friendliness, as of dwarfs shaking hands, was in
      the air:
the two men meeting for the first time, the one
      who had
carved "I love Felicia" on the desk top and
      the one
who had added "Me, too!" in smaller letters
      below. Each
was of normal height in the common sense, though each
      had been
dwarfed by his love for Felicia, of whom
      nothing was
known, not even if she existed except as
      a bond

between the two men, who may have made her up
      in order
to form a club dedicated to the word
      amor, love
perfect and unchanging, as though carved in precious
      stone and
hung on the breast of a beauty in a
      gallery, long
ago—that is to say, they met as giants,
      grotesque and
triumphant, and one didn't know whether to
      pity or
envy them or extend a hand and say, "I too
      loved her."

Ending in the Title of a Song by Harvey and the Moonglows (Chess Records, 1958)

That year Bobby Rodriguez started going out with
Cookie Stewart, who had just broken up
with Ronnie Carter, who was two years older
than we were, because, Cookie said,
Ronnie had pulled out his thing one night
and asked her to play with it.

If he had been a hood like Jimmy Quinn,
who one morning pulled the fire alarm,
was sent home, sneaked back into school
that afternoon and pulled it again, okay,
but Ronnie Carter was class president
and captain of the tennis team.

It was hard to take him seriously after that:
every time he got up to say something
at an assembly, you couldn't help but see him
sitting there in his dad's Plymouth,
pants open, thing sticking up in the air
like nothing on this earth.

Cookie told Bobby that if all men
were like that, she was never going
to marry one. She did, though,
years later, somebody
who wasn't from our school.
They have six kids, which means

there is more to heaven and earth
than was dreamt of in your philosophy,
Ronnie Carter: I see you at football games
from time to time, talking to other men,
and wonder if you ever learned
"The Ten Commandments of Love."

Virginia Rilke

Each day I park my car
        and walk through crowds
of girls and boys on their way to school.
        The girls, who laugh and kid each other,
talk about the boys
        but also their diets and other girls.
The boys, who are grim and unsmiling,
        talk about pussy
but also sports and the business courses
        they are taking.

I would like to upbraid these caballeros,
        to tell them something
about the sweetness of sexual love
        and the cruelty of words,
also the foolishness
        of thinking of women
in terms of conquest
        or cost efficiency
and how, in fact,
        the most improbable romances

are often the best.
        Suppose, for example,
that Virginia Woolf
        were to marry
what's his name—Rilke!
        King of the unreconciled polarity!
"Say to the still earth, I flow!
        Say to the rapid water, I am!"
Now that's fine writing.
        Then there's *Mrs. Dalloway*

and those other great novels:
        resonant forms, resonant forms!
Virginia, Virginia,
        you're my favorite Virginia.
You're Virginia Rilke now,
        the boys would say,
and I am a foolish fellow
        if I imagine
for a minute that Woolf,
        with her spells

of incapacitating and,
        at times, suicidal depression,
would make a suitable helpmeet
        for such a one as Rilke,
for whom the claims of marriage
        or indeed of any
demanding emotional relationship
        were irreconcilable
with his poetic vocation.
        To which I fancy myself replying,

Hoity toity, knaves—
        neither Leonard Woolf
not the sculptress Clara Westhoff
        were exactly what the doctor ordered
for Virginia and what's-his-name respectively,
        so why not each other
for each other?
        They would have been kind,
sweet, nervous, at least
        intermittently passionate,

and, in the long run,
        doomed, as who is not?
But during their time together

   they would have taken any number
of long, almost certainly stormy walks
    yet agreed that in each of us
the urge to be bad is strong
    and that love at its best
is often funny-strange
    and always funny-ha-ha.

The Museum of Desire

So much is there,
so much that someone wanted once,
that no one wants now.
And each of the visitors
is thinking of the thing
he loves least: the ugly child,
the sweetheart grown fat and stupid.
In this wing, the girl,
rich and unappreciated, who wants
nothing more than to resemble
her own portrait;
in that, the boy
who runs to catch the ball
and runs and runs
but does not catch it.
And in his office,
the curator, a man sunk
in age, in the depth of his sorrow,
his beautiful manners.
As he sips his coffee,
a light inside the cup
bathes his face;
it is the world,
and the world is burning.

Ode to Languor

My father and I are watching the opera *Susannah*,
      or at least I am, for my father has fallen
into a deep and dreamless slumber, the way

he always has. When I was young, he used
      to take me to the National Geographic Film
series on Wednesdays, and once,

as the Mud Men of New Guinea were shaking
      their spears at the camera, Johnny Taylor
(I was too self-conscious to sit with

anyone not my age) nudged me and said,
      "Look at that old man sleeping!" Forty
years later, I am almost an old man myself

and grateful for the quality of languor,
      almost certainly genetically transmitted.
Blessed parent! He is also the perfect

erotic role model, i.e., not. My father
      chased no skirts—after a while,
not even my mother's. When I think of

friends who have broken their hearts
      in the pursuit of unattainable women,
I am all the more grateful to my drowsy father.

Keats praised languor: easeful death was something
      he was more than half in love with,
though he didn't mean a passing like his own.

Keats wanted a death-in-art, a rich death,
      with a nightingale pouring forth its soul
as Susannah, wronged by the lustful elders,

pours forth hers, my eyes closing,
        my head bending toward that
of my dreamless father, this good man sleeping.

La Forza del Destino in the Tri-State Area

As I sit here listening to Verdi's opera,
which is one of his lesser ones
but a pretty good piece of work
no matter what the critics say,
I realize that I am going to spend
the rest of my life
in the Tri-State Area,
by which I mean not Florida, Georgia, and Alabama
or even New York, New Jersey, and Connecticut

but that combination of moods and ideas
in which childhood memories overlap
with the things I am doing at present
as well as whatever it is I am reading.
I feel so strongly about this
that I would say it's my destiny right now
to be thinking of the time
my parents took me to visit some friends
who lived below a couple named Fox,

and that even though I was old enough to know better,
still, I was more than a little anxious
about meeting those neighbors on the stairs
in their old-fashioned clothes,
eyes bulging slightly,
tongues hanging out like red neckties,
smiles more like leers than smiles;
should I pat their noses
or offer them some of my candy?

And while I am thinking
about how foolish I was as a child,
I am also planning to meet these same parents of mine
at the Grand Hotel in Point Clear, Alabama,

which I imagine to be an old, rather formal establishment
with a restaurant where they serve very good food,
and as I pack my bag,
I think about and pack as well my copy
of a book about different aspects of neurophysiology,

which is the kind of witty yet sensitive study
I would like to write myself someday.
Anyway, that is why I no longer have a foot
in both camps or agree that there are two sides
to any question or that every game is a toss-up
or that it takes only two to tango.
Freud was right: our lives aren't determined,
they're overdetermined,
and since that is how they are going to be

no matter how we feel about them,
maybe we should try to think nice or
at least interesting thoughts all the time
and be kind to the parents
who gave us our lives in the first place
and read books that will make us
not only smarter but more fun to be around.
Oh, and listen to as much music as possible:
the more forza, the better the destino.

Portrait of the Artist's Parents as Young Dogs

The home where my mother lives is full of women
who say they've "lost" their husbands,
   as though the men managed to squeeze under a fence
or dart through a gate someone had left open.
   Now they won't come when called,
and my own mother will have to phone
    the Humane Society to say,

Have you seen my husband, a quiet man,
   affectionate though not demonstrative?
The night before he died, my father asked my mother
   if there was any money left, and when she said there was,
he said let's get out of this place;
    when she answered that he couldn't walk
and she couldn't see, he said that's all right,

    we'll manage, let's just go.
Since then she says nothing seems real anymore
   and sometimes she says she wants to be where he is now,
though not dead, surely,
   and not in that awful hospital
where she saw him last,
    where she calls for the nurse and says,

When I touch his face, I can't feel anything,
   I don't think he's breathing anymore;
the nurse says, He's not,
   and *a couple of terriers slip through the door*
and break for the open. They race, tumble,
   spring up, nip each other's flanks,
tear across a sunny meadow together toward a dark wood.

A Flaccid Penis

It sows not, neither does it reap.
And the one to whom it does not respond
calls it impotent, as though
it should not discriminate,
should go where it is told,
do as it is commanded.

If that were so,
its owner would be a happier man.
Yet the flaccid penis itself is not unhappy,
is not dissatisfied with its appearance,
thinks of itself not as loathsome
because unmanly, unengorged, unred

but modest and unassuming, pink as a girl,
as well out of it
in its musky tent
as a heroine dreaming
of a cool bath in a marble tank,
in a darkened chamber, in a hot land.

The First Lovers

They didn't know what to do or how to do it,
but they talked it over as best they could:
pointing, smiling, showing the empty hands,
then windmilling their arms wildly

in anticipation of the unknowable,
the thing that would soon be theirs.
He had seen the baboons do it
and had even tried it with them once,

but the baboons wouldn't have him;
they chittered and puffed their chests
and then surged upward, the whole herd together,
disappeared like a wave into the trees.

And she had watched the fish and wondered
if it were harder for them because they had no legs
or easier since they were smooth all over and lacked parts,
at least parts that she could see.

They knew it was right when everything fit, above
as well as below. It took a while to work out the rhythm,
and once they stopped to check each other's hands again
to make sure they were still empty.

It wasn't much fun.
They were so excited and unsure of themselves
that they felt like the twins they had seen one day,
the one who was identical

and the one who didn't resemble anyone at all.
So that as they lay sleeping in each other's arms,
they dreamed of other sweethearts,
good ones this time, patient, more experienced.

And then they dreamed of us. We frightened them:
in their dreams we were taller than they were
and lightly haired. How ugly we were!
And how unhappy, because we weren't like them at all,

and everything we did was different, wrong.
The first lovers turned uneasily in their sleep,
and as they turned, they ate the meat of forgetfulness.
And when they woke, they didn't recognize themselves,

much less each other. And then they realized
what they had become: that they were the same
as they'd had always been, unavoidably,
but now they were new people as well, adorable strangers.

That was how the race began. And language:
sounds ballooned out of their mouths, risible at first,
then affecting. They composed songs for each other,
and poems, plays, thick squarish novels.

But they liked the old gestures best:
the smiles, the little caresses, the open hands
which still say, My life before I met you
was like this, it was this way, it was nothing.

The First Tax Collector

They couldn't figure out who he was or what he wanted
or why he wanted it from them—why not another village

where the hunt had been more successful
or some hamlet where the crops had come in big-time?

Why them with their greasy pots and their little handfuls
of roots and berries, not even picked over yet?

He kept smiling and said that everyone had to pay
and that the money wasn't for him, it was for his boss,

the king. King? said the people. King, king!
he said, the guy who lives behind that hill there,

and the tax collector jerked his thumb over his shoulder.
But the people still wanted to know why and he got mad

and said it was to pay for the things
they couldn't do themselves and they said like what

and he looked distracted for a minute and said
well, like collect taxes and they said oh, listen,

we tax ourselves all the time. We've given up so much
already, they said, you don't know the half of it.

First, each of us has suffered an irreversible loss;
it happened when we were born or just after.

Then every morning it's something else, and we end up
starving that we might eat, thirsting that we might drink:

the day breaks, things look pretty good, and then it's
starve, thirst, work for play that comes late, if ever.

And that's our lives. Yet out of affection,
out of good will, we make gestures of normalcy every day:

we vote, we marry, we have children, we join the PTA,
we keep our homes in good repair,

all the while thinking the whole deal faintly comical.
We *persist*, is the main thing. And now you want more?

Forget it, we won't be paying your taxes.
And the tax collector looked annoyed and said

Listen, you don't want me to whistle up my boys, do you?
He said you'll get used to it; the folks over in Bramble did,

and the ones in Rocktown are starting to see things our way.
But the people had heard enough, so they took the tax man out

and put him in a well. Then they coined the word "emissary."
Then they sent emissaries to Bramble and Rocktown

and encouraged them not to listen, not to pay.
And the king didn't get any taxes that year.

The following year, there was no king.
Yet the people taxed themselves and put a good face on it,

and after a while they began to wonder what it would be like
to give up everything. There would be nothing left

but their names and the names of the towns they lived in
and, after a while, not even that.

The people would live the way the animals do:
empty, naked, quiet, poor.

So they did it. They gave it all away,
all except the one thing that comforted them the most

when they couldn't feed themselves or were so filthy
that the dirt felt like their own skin.

We have to hang on to something! said one old man,
and some of the young rowdies agreed with him.

Then punches were thrown, the miller's nose was bloodied,
and almost everyone said something they didn't really believe.

But a woman, speaking softly, explained what
they all knew to be true, so that the old man was persuaded,

and while the young rowdies grumbled, finally they too said
Yeah, it would be best if there were nothing left,

not even the resentment they'd all wrapped themselves in
on cold nights or bitten savagely

like a piece of bread someone might find
at the bottom of a sack she'd sworn was empty.

Little Stabs of Happiness

The night Sam Cooke was shot,
I ran out into the back yard
and shouted, "Suck my dick, God!"
My father slapped my face,
said if he ever heard me
say anything like that again,
I could forget about driving, ever—
I'd be in my own house
with my own kids
and he'd show up
to take away the car keys.
Like I cared:
Sam Cooke was dead.

Every time I hear Sam Cooke's voice
on the radio, I feel these little stabs
of happiness, then a grief so profound
I've had to pull over to the side
of the road and gasp for breath,
my face in my hands
like Jerome in his hermit's cave
after Alaric sacked Rome
and "the light had gone out of the world."
Poor me! The knives of joy slash and chop.
There's nowhere to go,
my car's too small,
yet I'm happy!
Crowded and happy!
And miserable also.
Sam Cooke, you send me,
honest you do.

The Gigolo in the Gazebo

There is a gigolo in the gazebo, Mother,
worrying about the weather:
someone was buried in the base of the gazebo,
and now a cloud is passing over the moon,
and rain may wash away the flagstones and cement,
said to be poorly mixed, leaving the gigolo
with a body and no alibi, since Mrs. Alfred Uruguay
will never admit to having been with him
in the boudoir or even the foyer, much less the gazebo.

Mrs. Alfred Uruguay thinks the gigolo fancies himself
and is fearful of indiscretion; she doesn't know
he is so distracted that he can't decide
whether to relight his cheroot or take out another.
Now he smooths his brillantined hair and pauses—
was it he who put the body in the base of the gazebo?
And what to do with his hands? In the parlor,
he could wipe them on any antimacassar,
but now he is alone in the gazebo. Solo,

the gigolo would like to have a split of Veuve Cliquot
sent 'round. He wishes he were a thinking stone
or one of the first white men in the mountains
of New Guinea so that he could make the natives cry,
"Here comes the man from heaven in his evening clothes,
his boiled shirt!" The gigolo wishes someone would
land in, not just any biplane, but a De Haviland Foxmoth
to take him away from Mrs. Alfred Uruguay and from
his present ennui and away from the body under the gazebo.

Bottomless Cup

The best thing in the world is coffee,
especially the cup I have first thing
every day, three scoops of espresso
and one of American coffee with chicory,
filtered. Around town it's commercially
prepared and lousy, but I drink it anyway
in honor of that first cup, which makes
the subsequent ones not so bad,
and because I love the stuff.
Of course various hosts and hostesses
in this city make very serviceable coffee
after the dinners to which I am often
invited, having something of a reputation
as a useful hand in the kitchen
and more than passable conversationalist,
but by then it's too late in the evening
for good coffee, which only disturbs sleep,
thus dulling one's appreciation
of that matutinal cup, the first one,
every day! It's silly to get caught up

in rituals, I know, but a friend told me
his father recovered from his mother's death
by taking up again the little routines
he'd practiced daily, all his life.
So coffee might save me from despair
one of these days, since I certainly
don't expect to go through
without my share of blows. Well, you see,
that ruins it; now all this coffee-drinking
has a purpose, which it shouldn't.
I don't even need the stuff to wake up with,
being fairly jumpy most of the time anyway.
I suppose I drink it because I want

to be more like coffee myself,
the thing people need when they get up
in the morning and then all day long,
something even the poor can afford.
I want to find myself everywhere.
I want to be the thing that's bad for you
if you get too much.

II

There was always something supernatural about him. Elvis was a force of nature. Other than that he was just a turd. A big dumb hillbilly a couple points smarter than his mule who wandered out from behind his plow one day to cut a record for his sainted mother and never came back, which he probably woulda forgot to do even if he hadn't have been whisked up. Why shouldn't one physical corpus be capable of containing these two seeming polarities simultaneously?

—music critic Lester Bangs

The Potato Mash
(More Indefinite and More Soluble)

If Debussy had written the score to the story of my adolescence,
  he would have called it, after the name of the poem
by his good friend Mallarmé, *L'Après-Midi d'un Dope.*
  So many adventures! All of them stupid.
For a while I worked for a rock band;
  I handled the bookings, the equipment, and the snacks.
The band leader played the French horn,
  which is all he knew how to play;
it was the only rock and roll French horn in the business.

And the bassist, who had never played at all,
just hit whatever notes he felt like hitting,
  saying it didn't make any difference
because nobody ever paid any attention to the bass line anyway.
  Then there were the two blind brothers,
a drummer and a guitarist,
  good musicians who drank bourbon and ate doughnuts
during the shows, always with disastrous results,
  though the band was horrible to begin with.

We never accomplished our goal of meeting pliant women,
  and everywhere we went,
the drunken fishermen we played for were mad at us
  because our music had not brought out any women for them.
Instead we played songs like "The Mashed Potatoes,"
  each time to a smaller and surlier crowd.
We "loosened classical tonality" the way Debussy did,
  and at times we destroyed it, like Schoenberg,
when the blind boys were too far gone.

Our last night, I knew it was going to be bad;
one of the customers had stopped me coming back
  from the men's room to ask why I didn't use hair tonic.

Then a big guy in suspenders and a plaid shirt
    and a cap that said "Sex is like snow,
you never know how many inches you're going to get"
    came up to the bandstand and asked,
"Y'all can play dat Potato Mash?"
    We knew our career was over anyway,

so we began to laugh and make fun of him,
    and he and his friends jumped up on stage
to throw beer at us and turn over the drum kit.
    The three of us who could see were frightened
by these hairy bayou men with their great hard bellies
    and their forearms big as Popeye's,
but the blind boys didn't give a shit
    and were ripped on bourbon and doughnuts anyway;
howling, their fish-belly eyes red in the light

from the beer signs, the blind boys lashed out
and began to hit the men and us and each other
    with the neck of the guitar and the drum sticks.
It was a fight in hell: "The Musicians versus the Fisherman,"
    like a myth from some country that had never developed
much of a culture. I got a cut lip and my first real hangover,
    and for days my parents heaped shame on my silent head.
But it was worth it to have seen the blind boys
    whip the ass of those tough fisherman;

for sure, they did the Potato Mash. Later we got more bourbon
    and more doughnuts and had a real party.We sang and threw up,
and one of the blind boys cried for his mother.
    That was our only good moment—our last. On the ride home,
we were a lyrical and pantheistic group of fellows,
    and our music was *plus vague et plus soluble dans l'air,*
according to the formula of the poet Verlaine,
    son-in-law of Madame Mauté de Fleurville,
Debussy's first teacher and herself a student of Chopin.

The Flesh Eaters

I came across another people who were anthropophagous: the
ugliness of their features says so.
> —C. Colón, *Textos y documentos completos*

1 *The Crew, With Less Fear Than Wonder*

> A race of ugly folk without heads
> who have eyes in each shoulder,
> headless people with mouths and noses
> on their backs, ugly fellows
> with upper lips so big that when
> they sleep in the sun they cover
> all their faces with it,
> a race whose ears hang down
> to the ground, hermaphrodites
> whose male side begets children
> and whose female side bears them,
> a people with a single foot
> that shades them when they lie
> on their backs, a people who live on
> the smell of one kind of apple,
> and if they have not that smell,
> they die: these things were written of
> by good Sir John Mandeville
> in his celebrated *Travels*.

2 *Chipangu, A Large Island of the East Described by Marco Polo and
Later Called Japan*

<pre>
            Hum, hey!   Hum!
                        Messer Colón!   can it be
    The Great Khan   there he is!   hey
                                                 This way!
            No, no—this way!
</pre>

3 Fernando, Son of the Very Magnicent Lord Don Cristobal Colón, Grand Admiral of the Ocean Sea

In his youth my father was a mariner but also a madcap, pause. Once a Genoese merchant fleet in which he sailed was attacked by a pirate called Coullon the Elder. The slaughter was terrible: men threw themselves into the waves rather than suffer the pain of their wounds. Pause, pause. My father's ship burned to the waterline and he swam six miles to shore; when he crawled onto the beach, he was a new man. As he regained his health, he conceived of a plan to get gold from the Great Khan written of by Marco Polo and raise armies to take back the Holy Sepulchre from the Saracens. Pause. He seldom smiled after that day.

4 The Ancient Cartographers on the Presence of Hippogriffs and Anthropophagi on the Borders of Their Maps

Where you know nothing, place terrors.

5 Fernando, Son of, Etc.

On the evening of September 25th, 1492, Martin Pinzón shouted from the poop of the *Pinta* that he had sighted Chipangu, but the next day the sea was empty. Pause. The three ships finally touched land, but my father kept searching for Chipangu, which the natives called Colba, then Caniba, then Ciabo, pause. My father did considerable naming of islands himself, often changing them to accord with a name used by Marco Polo, so that Yamaye, for instance, became Yanahica. Some of the men said that the great discoverer was not fond of discovery.

6 *Anacaona, A Carib Woman of Exceptional Beauty*

One of Colón's lieutenants
tried to have his way with me
but I treated him so with my nails
that he wished he had never begun.

Then he took a piece of rope
and whipped me so soundly
that I came to terms with him
to save myself from death.

Later he told the others
I was so lively
he would have thought
I had been brought up

in a school for whores,
but even as I gave myself
I bit and scratched and twisted,
for I was fighting him.

7 *Fernando the Son*

Pause. In his later voyages my father's distemper was even more pronounced. He went for thirty-two nights without sleep one time and imagined himself in a sea white as milk with three figures walking toward him across the water, emissaries of the Great Khan. Another day he decided that the sea had disappeared and that his boats were sailing through a colossal field of yellow corn. Once he thought he was in Paradise, pause. Yet always he sought Chipangu.

8 *The Crew, With As Much Fear As Wonder This Time*

It rained. It rained.
Yet a strange fire surrounded us.

And a waterspout came down
from the sky to cast us about
like toothpicks. But the Admiral
read from the Gospel of St. John
and traced crosses in the sky
with his sword while the waters
grew still and the sky quiet.

9 *Chipangu, With Unmistakable Irony*

Hum, hum!   Messer Colón!
    Over here, Messer Colón!   This way
  to the gold   good Messer
      gold for blue beads!   Hum!
Oh, the greedy Moor!
    Oh   hum   the nasty, greedy grabber!

10 *Fernando*

Once some men were brought to camp with pieces of flesh missing
from their bodies, and my father was given to understand that
cannibals had eaten mouthfuls of them, though he did not believe
this. Yet something had torn away the skin and muscle of these
creatures—what? The Admiral died repentant of much that he had
done, though he was not dishonored. Pause. Not wholly dishonored.
Pause, pause. Not in Valladolid.

Pain

I am sitting astride the partition
   at the back of the bar,
  my legs dangling on either side,
and the atmosphere is charged,
though it shouldn't be:
   tonight's reader is going on,
  in a manner neither convincing nor original,
about some bones he has found in the desert
   and how they have given him
  intimations of mortality,
while a tiny piece of my leg, high and on the inside,
has gotten into a space in the partition
   where two of the boards meet
  at a forty-five degree angle.

A big handsome fellow comes in late,
leans against the partition
   I am sitting on,
  and brings the boards together.
I sink my teeth into my lip
and whip my head from side to side
   like somebody faking orgasm
  in a cheap movie;
to my left, a girl working
on her extra-credit report writes,
   "Stinks and is boring"
  and arches an eyebrow at me
as if to say,
What's the big deal?

   I have seen strange things in bars.
 I have seen men so drunk they can't talk
and others so beside themselves with devilry
that they have to pull the condom machines

off the bathroom wall
or pick fights with scar-faced giants,
and once I saw a pretty blonde
ask two young studs
   if she could borrow their ashtray,
   and they lunged for it so hard
that they hit their heads together;
the pretty woman laughed
   and flicked her ashes on the floor
   as the studs rolled about and wept with pain.

I myself have been punched
more times than I care to remember,
   but words have made me more miserable than blows.
   Once I read "Dover Beach" to a class,
and years later, a student told me
she had gone home and cried
   because Arnold's world was so tragic
   and she decided then and there
to do the one thing that would set it right,
so she married her husband,
   a man who became an English professor himself
   and who had just left her,
having seduced a student of his own
with the same poem.

   The man on stage is reading something
   about an animal he saw by the side of the road
and how he realized that life was short,
and I am straining to pull the boards apart
   and get my leg out and not scream
   and the big handsome fellow
turns and scowls at me
because I am disturbing him
   and I finally succeed
   and the boards come together

with an audible click
and I can feel my flesh swelling
   as I think to myself,
    One way or the other, poetry is going to hurt you.

El Libro de Buen Amor

Here's how my mother taught me to dance;
  also, how she saved me from some bad whores—I mean cops!
Well, I don't know what they were. It happened this way:
  I am standing outside my motel in the Buckhead region
of Atlanta, waiting, as the song says, not on a lady
  but on a friend, having discussed the Tyson-Ruddock fight
ad nauseam with my man Darryl the security guard

        and even making a small bet, when a van pulls up
  and the two young women inside motion me over.
Would I like a date? they ask. Date? I reply, date?
  No, thanks, no dates, not tonight, I say,
as polite as my mother always taught me to be to everybody,
  yet curious, eager, even, to find out more
        about such women and their "dates," so I start

        to stick my head in their window and chat them up
  when I hear a voice say, "Don't do it, darling—they're cops!"
And there, on the balcony, between the ice maker
  and the soft drink machine, glowing fluorescently and hovering
maybe six inches off the ground, is an elderly woman,
  very familiar, hands raised in warning.
        I'm staring, you bet, and thinking, cops?

        I see the bad men of Atlanta suspended by their testicles
  from the streetlights like the crucified slaves
in *Spartacus* who line the road to Rome . . . .
  Just then my man Darryl appears to collect on the wager,
but he, too, freezes, transfixed by the eldritch vision;
  his eyes bug out of his head as he stammers, "It is
thy m-m-mother's spirit; / Doomed for a certain term to walk

        the night, and for the day confined to fast in fires . . . ,"
  but I interrupt because it really is my mother,

or at least that aspect of her which is alive in me
   and looks out for my best interests,
the part that has me dancing just beyond the reach
   of *les filles de joie* and those cops as well,
            my pelvis juking now, my hips swivelling skinny and fast.

            I shake my money-maker, I shimmy and slide;
   tearing away from bug-eyed Darryl, I samba down Piedmont
                        Avenue
while the bubbas of Buckhead rush from their lairs to cry,
   "Go, man, go!" and "Don't he dance good!"
I dance to defy the whores and the crummy cops, too,
   my fanny pumping left and right as they claw at me,
            their hoarse howls splitting the air over Atlanta,

but mainly I am dancing for that wise woman
   my mother who, when I was born, wrapped me in a blanket
first thing and fed me and then wrote my name
   in the Book of Good Love—to her,
the daughters of joy are hapless, to be sure,
   but those cops are something else altogether,
            i. e., abandoned by God.

The Birth and Untimely Death of the Musical Legacy of the Outlaw Jesse James

Carl Sandburg's immigrant father worked six days
  a week as a blacksmith's helper for fourteen cents
an hour and spent everything he earned
  on his family except for the occasional nickel
he gave to a street musician who'd sing the ballad
  of Jesse James. August Sandburg would request

"de Yesse Yames song" and drop his coin
  in the guy's cup. The singer'd torture his instrument
for a minute, then: some people say he crazy,
  some people say he insane. A-whoo gawd,
some people say the singer crazy, some say
  he insane. But he don't care about

nothing (have mercy) 'cept that old Jesse James.
  Hot damn! August Sandburg's been zapped
by the music's wounding joy. He throws
  his cap down and "cuts loose" right there
on the Galesburg sidewalk; wagging his calloused
  forefingers in the air, he shouts, "De beauty's

still on duty, y'all! De beauty's still on duty!"
  Because Jesse James was nobody's fool
and nobody's helper; he was his own boss
  and set his own wages. He was the first rock star,
like Elvis, only earlier and less fake.
  Imagine JFK in the months before he killed himself;

it's the summer of 1963, and he's lying
  on the White House floor thinking about
the Yesse Yames song and sharing a little reefer
  with one of Sam Giancana's tomatoes,
and that darned Caroline, cute as a puppy
  yet always fooling with the dial,

has left the radio tuned to one
  of those freaky rock stations. JFK hears the drums
on Bobby Freeman's "Do You Wanna Dance";
  they sound like somebody slapping
a wet cardboard box with an ax handle,
  and suddenly he's zapped, too;

he's prissing around like August Sandburg,
  he's writhing like Henry Adams before the dynamo
in the Gallery of Machines at the Great
  Exposition of 1900, "historical neck broken
by the sudden irruption of forces totally new."
  JFK gets up and he thinks, Fuck Sinatra

and he says, "I want to hear the Yesse Yames song"
  or he wants to be the singer of the Yesse Yames song
or be Yesse Yames himself. I'll fix Castro's ass
  once I'm the outlaw Yesse Yames, you betcha!
Or maybe you fixed it already, jefe:
  sometimes it's hard to remember

if you did what you did or if you just got it
  mixed up with all the songs you've ever heard.
Now it's November 22—crawling past
  the Texas Book Depository, the limo driver
is looking for some good tunes but accidentally
  dials up Elvis singing "Bossa Nova Baby,"

recorded earlier that same year,
  JFK grabs the Secret Service guy's gun
and shoots himself in the head rather than go on living
  in a world that plays such crappy music.
Elvis kills the president! Elvis goes to jail!
  Elvis needs to go to jail anyway

for selling out August Sandburg,
  for betraying Yesse Yames,
and for killing off rock and roll itself
  nine years earlier, in December 1954,
raw power turning to Vegas horsecrap in the
  false start to "Milkcow Blues Boogie,"

where he says, "Hold it, fellas. That don't move.
  Let's get real, real gone." But future president
Richard M. Nixon will need Elvis as a kiss-ass stoolie
  during his own administration, so he pays
phony desperado Lee Oswald to take the fall,
  what a chump.

III

Because the way our shows used to work—well, they didn't work at all actually.

—Jerry Garcia

The Summer of the Cuban Missile Crisis

Dickie asked if we were hungry, and Art and I
  said yeah, sure, so he pulled into the Walt Whitman
Service Plaza near Camden and there, in front
  of the very Howard Johnson's where we planned to eat,
was a bus with painted fire blazing down its sides
  and above it, in letters two feet high, the words
JAMES BROWN AND THE FAMOUS FLAMES, and I thought,
  righhht, this is it: I am sixteen years old,

I have my first paying job, I'm traveling across country
  with two guys who are older and cooler than I am
yet who seem to accept me as their equal,
  and now I'm going to meet Mr. I Got You, Mr. Let a Man
Get Up and Do the Popcorn (Part I), Mr. I Break Out
  in a Cold Sweat, the Hardest Working Man
in Show Business, James Brown himself.

Dickie was Dickie Biles, and Art was Arthur Kennedy,
  and they both went to the LSU Medical School
in New Orleans, so it was no problem for them
  to swing through Baton Rouge on their way
to Massachusetts and give me a ride to the camp
  where we'd all been hired to work that summer,
even though they were the camp doctors and I was
  just a kid and a mere archery/riflery counselor at that.

Dickie was not only full of ideas and fun
  but was also one of those people who knows someone
in every town, so that whenever we got tired
  or hungry, we'd pull over, Dickie would get out
his address book, and within five minutes, we'd be
  turning into the driveway of one of his friends,
including a guy in Lynchburg, Virginia

named Stump who'd just finished a pizza and a six pack
   when Dickie called and who kept staring at Dickie
in disbelief and asking me and Art,
   "What did you say your names were?"
Then there was Dickie's friend in Arlington
   who had a beagle who sang along when Dickie
played the piano, and a third friend in Chevy Chase,
   Maryland who had played bagpipes for the Trinity College

Drum & Fife Corps and who said, "Watch this,
   the neighbors hate it" and went into his back yard
and lit into "McPherson's Lament" or something like that,
   and sure enough, all these old people came out
of their houses and said, "Now cut that out" and
   "That's it, I'm calling the cops"—pretty heady stuff
for a provincial sixteen-year-old, but nothing

compared to the prospect of meeting Mr. Try Me,
   Mr. Stand Up I Feel Like a Sex Machine,
Mr. Please, Please, Please, the unquestioned King
   of Rhythm and Blues. Of course, he wasn't there:
JB had gone ahead, probably by limo, but the Famous Flames
   were all inside the Howard Johnson's, waiting
for their food to come and looking extremely hip
   in their shiny suits and skinny ties. Dickie and Art

and I sat at the counter and placed our orders—I remember
   having a chicken salad on toast and a strawberry soda made
with peppermint ice cream—but while we were waiting
   for our food, a guy sitting a few stools down from us
began to pitch a fit. "This malted tastes terrible,"
   he said, only he pronounced it "mwalted,"
and he held up his malt glass and waved it

at the counter girl, who was about my age and
  extremely pretty, and said, "There's something wrwong heh,
something very wrwong," and he kept waving the glass
  at the counter girl and trying to get her to taste
the malt, and by now she was nearly in tears,
  and the guy was kicking up such a ruckus
that even the Famous Flames had stopped being cool
  and were looking our way. It was probably just

a soapy glass, if anything, but the guy was making
  such a fuss that finally Dickie got up and went over
to him and said, "Richard Biles, M. D."
  (which wasn't quite true, since he still had a year
of medical school left), "may I see that glass, please?
  Hmm, yes. Yes," said Dickie, sniffing the malt
suspiciously, "it's as I feared." Then he put one thumb

on the guy's eyelid and peered in. "Sir, you have
  been poisoned. Someone has put poison in your
malted milkshake. And there is no cure."
  The guy stared at Dickie for a second, eyes bulging
with terror, and went, "Gaaahh!" and ran out into
  the parking lot, clutching his neck with both hands.
The counter girl burst out laughing, and so did
  the Famous Flames, who gave each other

complicated handshakes and told Dickie
  he was all right and autographed a Howard Johnson's
place mat for me, and as we went out the door,
  I looked back, and the counter girl had put a little kiss
on her finger tips and she blew it at me, but I was so
  surprised that I didn't catch it and berated myself
later for having been so clumsy and stupid,

and off we went to Cape Namequoit in Orleans, Massachusetts,
   where Dickie and Art passed out aspirin and bandaids
and calamine lotion, and I taught kids
   not to shoot themselves and even to hit the target
from time to time, and the summer went by in a hazy blur,
   the best thing about it having already happened
at the very beginning. Now obviously
   I still think about those days a lot, but when I do,

I think less of Dickie Biles and the Famous Flames
   and the poisoned guy and the pretty counter girl
and more of Art Kennedy, who was one of those big,
   bearish men whose solid calm was a welcome contrast
to Dickie's excitability and my provincial self-doubt
   and who never said much the whole trip but looked out
the window a lot and whom I now associate with the other,

more celebrated Kennedys: John and Bobby, who would be
   shot dead in a few years, and tragic, lucky Teddy,
who would let poor Mary Jo Kopechne drown in a pond not far
   from where the camp where we worked and then go scot free,
whereas anyone else would have done serious time.
   There was something in Art's gaze as he looked out
of Dickie's car window, and the shadows grew long,
   and the sun went down over Lynchburg and Arlington

and Chevy Chase. The summer sped by more quickly
   than anyone could have imagined, and with it came
the Cuban missile crisis and, soon, rumors
   about John and Marilyn, and then Oswald and
the grassy knoll and the Freedom Riders the summer
   after that, and then the war and hippies and acid
and the Summer of Love, and then rumors

about Bobby and Marilyn, and then Sirhan Sirhan
  and Malcolm X and the police riots in Chicago
and the three days of Woodstock and the bridge
  at Chappaquiddick, all of it springing from
that sad, gaudy amalgam of touch football and nooky
  and Harvard diplomas and boat races off Hyannisport
and conspiracies and mob connections
  and horsedrawn carriages going up Pennsylvania Avenue

to the sound of muffled drums. What I tell myself
  is that Art was the brother who got away,
who deliberately turned his back on that whole bright,
  shining family, its blood hot with poison even
in those innocent days, though no one could have known it
  at the time. He was the smart Kennedy, the one who didn't
say anything because he knew no one would believe him.

Lurch, Whose Story Doesn't End

It's like you're snowed in at the airport forever.
  Or you're sent to purgatory, say:
you spend all this time learning the story of your own life
  and then you don't get to tell it.
This one begins with me and the other guys
  carrying stuff into our half of the house
we had rented for spring break,
  while Whit Little takes his clothes off on the beach,
folds them carefully, and walks into the waves.
  A few minutes later, the girls pull up in their car.
They have their swimsuits on under their blouses and shorts,
  so they took off their clothes off, too,
and run down to the water as Whit smiles
  and greets them, his hands on his hips.

Whit, Whit! they scream. How's the water?
  Great, you'll love it, he replies.
Just then the tide goes out with a great sucking roar,
  and Whit is left in water up to his ankles,
his nuts tight from the chill
  and his big, floppy, half-hard penis
sticking out like an elephant's trunk.
  Sondra Broussard, who is in front, digs in her heels;
the other girls scream and crash into her and fall
  in a big heap on the sand. Then they run back up
the beach again, still screaming but laughing now,
  and put their girl stuff into their half of the house
we'd all rented together in Grayton Beach,
  half a day's drive from Baton Rouge.

That night there is a poker game in the kitchen.
  Maybe Lurch is one of the card players;
if that were the case, his story would begin here,
  but I can't remember where he first comes in.

The girls spin records and dance in the living room
   except for Kathey Smiley, who sits and watches the poker game,
not saying anything. Kathey doesn't look so great;
   she'd been on the beach all day in her two-piece,
refusing everyone's offer of lotion because,
   as she kept saying, she was going to get
the "basis" of a tan first and then
   start smearing on the Coppertone later.
She'd been light pink at supper
   and by now she is a deep red, bordering on purple.

Around one, most of the girls have gone to bed ,
   and the guys are tired of the beer and the cards,
so we get up to go to our rooms, everybody but Kathey,
   who just sits there. Come on, Kathey, bedtime,
say the guys, See you tomorrow, come on, get up, get up.
   I can't, says Kathy, and everybody stops,
and the guys who have left the room come back.
   What? says someone. I can't get up, says Kathy,
I can't move, and she begins to cry.
   There is a quick discussion, and then the Wilkersons,
two pairs of brothers who are also cousins
   and who played football together in high school,
get on the four corners of Kathey Smiley's chair.
   One, two, three, says somebody,

and the four Wilkersons lift Kathey Smiley up,
   chair and all, and take her out
to Robby Wilkerson's truck, the bed of which
   had been filled that morning with cans of tomato soup
and boxes of evaporated milk and jars of peanut butter
   and loaves of white bread and case after case of beer
but which is now empty.
   And so we take Kathey Smiley
to the Okaloosa County Regional Medical Center,
   where she spends the next ten days

on painkillers. Kathey finally comes around,
   but it's long after we'd all driven back to Baton Rouge
and returned to our classes at LSU
   and our regular boy- and girlfriends.

And that could be the end of a story,
   though not the story of Lurch,
since he hasn't even appeared yet,
   except perhaps as one of the nameless guys,
the one who says What? to Kathey Smiley, for example,
   or who signals for the Wilkersons to pick her up.
Surely there's enough for a story already:
   there's Whit Little and his big semi-hard dick,
then the serious matter of Kathey Smiley's burns,
   and, finally, Kathey's eventual recovery.
Lots of stories work this way:
   with the joke (Whit), the big scare
(Kathey gets severely burned) and then
   the brow-wiping moment of relief (Kathey gets better).

It would be the story of a day
   in the life of some nice middle-class kids,
half of whose names I've long since forgotten.
   I don't think anyone married anyone else in the group,
although most of them did marry and have children,
   and a good many divorced and probably drank too much
on occasion and fudged on their taxes
   but otherwise had lives much like the day
we had all just passed together,
   lives with some ups but some downs, too,
some levity and some pain, yet nothing
   nobody couldn't get over.
The story so far is their story,
   and it's probably *the* story for most people.

But it wouldn't be Lurch's story if it ended here.
   Lurch hasn't even appeared yet, and it would've been better
if he hadn't appeared at all, if he'd been one
   of the ones whose names I can't remember.
In fact, Lurch got into and then out of the story
   without me knowing it. I'd gone to the hospital
with Kathey Smiley and the Wilkersons;
   someone was needed in the truck bed
to hold the fourth leg of Kathy's chair
   so Robby Wilkerson could drive to the hospital.
Naturally we thought the story had gone with us,
   but when we got back to the house in Grayton Beach,
we found the story was still there
   and had been all along.

All the lights in the house were on;
   the house was so brightly lit
that it looked as though it were on fire.
   And everyone was walking around outside,
either crying or vomiting. One of the guys,
   Bob Fisher, had been drinking all day long
and had begun to lie down in front of cars
   as they bounced along the little beach road.
He'd pretend he was an accident victim,
   and when the drivers got out to see if they could help,
he'd cackle and lurch off into the bushes.
   In fact, we called him Lurch after the character
on *The Addams Family*, since he was also big
   and ungainly and had a low voice.

As the Wilkersons and I took Kathey
   to the hospital, some of the other guys
decided to follow us, so they piled into
   Greg Cangelosi's jeep and took off.
Lurch, who was quite drunk by now,
   ran down the road a little bit, hid in the bushes,

and flopped down in front of the jeep;
   in all the excitement, Greg didn't see him
and, in fact, didn't even know he'd run over him
   until one of the guys looked back
and saw Lurch lying there with his legs broken
   and his chest crushed.
And that's the scene we came back to
   after we'd taken Kathey to the hospital.

That's the problem with the story of Lurch,
   because it's the last thing I remember:
the unnatural light that streamed out of the house,
   and everybody outside, crying or vomiting.
Obviously the police were brought in,
   and Lurch's body was taken somewhere,
probably to the hospital where Kathy was lying,
   coming in and out of consciousness
and thinking during her wakeful moments
   that the story was still there with her.
And Lurch's parents must have been notified,
   and surely somebody led a prayer at the beach,
and there must have been a funeral
   when we got back to Baton Rouge again.

But all I remember is the chaos
   and the bright, hazy pain
that streamed from the windows
   of the house in Grayton Beach
and then nothing; the next thing I knew,
   I was sitting in class again,
trying to make sense of what my teachers were saying
   and wondering whether I should keep going out
with the girl I'd been dating.
   She was really pretty, but she was getting
more and more sarcastic all the time,
   so I was thinking of asking out a girl

I sat next to in The Eighteenth-Century Novel
    who was plainer but had a better disposition.

So, on the one hand, it was as though
    nothing had happened. On the other,
the worst thing that could have happened, did.
    I'm still not sure where the story of Lurch begins.
All I'm sure of is the bright, painful middle,
    the house with that horrible light coming out of it,
and everybody out front, sobbing and throwing up.
    And it's obvious that the story can't end there,
sans dénouement, as it were. But if I'm not sure
    where the story of Lurch begins,
maybe it doesn't have to have an ending.
    Or maybe some stories simply don't end.
Certainly the story of Lurch never ends;
    it just stops being told.

AFEES

During the Vietnam War, I had a hard time figuring out
exactly what to do, because I was opposed to the violence,
but while the peace rallies and parades were a lot of fun,
meanwhile the war just kept going on, and people were dying
on both sides. Then I got the idea of becoming
a draft counselor, which was a way of helping others
while I helped myself, since I neither wanted to go to Canada
nor, as a friend of mine had, stick a firecracker up my butt.

You don't have to do anything, he said; you just stick it
up there, and when they give you your physical, they'll say,
What're you doing with that firecracker up your butt,
and you can say, What firecracker or My mommy put it there,
and the next thing you know, you're on the bus heading home.
I couldn't do it, though. I didn't want to live in Canada,
yet I couldn't equate the idea of sticking a firecracker up
my butt with anything I could call a serious political act.

So I took the draft-counselor training and started doing it.
A lot of the guys I counseled were really hateful,
because, while they were all for the war, they didn't want to go
themselves, and clearly they thought I was a sissy or
a communist for being a draft counselor, though they
certainly didn't mind me helping them to stay in the States with
their custom cars and their pliant, resentful girlfriends
while their buddies went over to get shot at and die.

But there were a lot of nice fellows, too,
and I was proud to help them stay out of the Army,
especially the ones who were poor and black
and therefore most likely to end up there.
The main thing I learned was to leave a paper trail,
that the Army loved paper and would rather believe
a laughable story that was backed up by a couple of pounds
of files than a weighty one with nothing to substantiate it.

I myself suffered from asthma, and when I found out it would
keep me out of the army, because who wants soldiers who
        wheeze
and turn blue when they should be charging up hills in full
    combat gear, I thought, great! I don't have to go, either!
        It was a simple matter of writing my family doctor and
getting a photocopy of my records, which I did. It was a good
thing, too, because shortly thereafter I received a summons to my
    local Armed Forces Examination and Entrance Station or AFEES.

        The acronym disquieted me, because AFEES sounded vaguely
    like "feces," which, in an aggressive all-male environment,
led me to thoughts of unwanted penetration—not rape, exactly,
    but something along the line of my annual prostate exam.
        Once I complained to my doctor about him
    sticking his finger up there every August,
and he said, Well, you know, David,
        it's not exactly my favorite part of the day, either.

        But at AFEES, I was afraid it just might be
    their favorite part of the day, so even though
I was confident I would beat the draft, I really
    didn't want to go, not that I had much say about it
        at that point. So my father drove me down to the Post Office
at six a. m. one July morning, and I got on a bus with
a bunch of other Baton Rouge boys to be transported
    to AFEES, which was in New Orleans.

        Like me, the other fellows had a bag
    with a change of clothing and a toothbrush,
since we'd all received the sinister warning that,
    even though the process only took a few hours normally,
        any of us was liable to be detained if necessary
    for further examination. My seatmate was a hippy
who had deliberately gone without bathing for two weeks.
        He also told me he had tried to deafen himself

the night before by lying on the floor
with his stereo speakers pressed against his ears
as he listened to his Iron Butterfly and Big Brother albums.
As we talked, he said, "Huh?" and "What?" a lot,
but I think he was just practicing for the army doctors,
because several times he responded to things
I said in a normal conversational voice
and which he obviously heard perfectly well.

I know one other boy on the bus, and that was Brody Saxon,
who had actually lived down the street from me
when we were kids and who, I knew for a fact,
had asthma that was much more severe than mine,
though when I asked him if he'd brought
his doctor's file, he looked at me blankly
and then shrugged and said,
Nah, I'll just tell them about it.

AFEES was on Canal Street, and when we got off the bus,
the shoppers were already piling into Maison Blanche
and D. H. Holmes, and for a moment I hated them, since
they were going to buy ties and loafers while
we were going to be sorted like cattle on their way
to the slaughterhouse. Inside, the sergeants
took away our stuff and made us strip to our underwear
and stand shoulder-to-shoulder in a long line.

A doctor appeared at one end of the line
and donned a rubber glove and I thought,
Uh-oh, here comes the AFEES part. "Gentleman,"
said a sergeant, "Put your hands on your hip."
Without moving his mouth, Brody Saxon, who was something
of a wag, said, "And let your backbone slip,"
echoing the song "Land of a Thousand Dances"
as performed by Mr. Wilson Pickett.

We examinees broke up. We were pretty nervous already,
   and probably anything would have done it,
but at any rate, we guffawed and pounded each other
   and fell out of formation, which drove the sergeants crazy.
   They ran around screaming at us as though
   we were in the army already, and for the rest of the day,
they were pretty rough on us for laughing
   at Brody's joke and otherwise showing disrespect for them,

   even though, as far as I was concerned, they were
   determined basically to kill us and not much else.
At one point I saw the hippy behind a plate-glass window
   in the room where they gave the hearing tests;
   he was smiling and shrugging and pointing at his ears
   while the doctors scowled and looked at the floor,
and then later I heard him "talking crazy,"
   although, instead of sounding like a real schizophrenic,

   he just said "wlaah" and "bluhh" and made childish faces
   whenever they asked him questions.
By now the seriousness of the whole thing
   was beginning to dawn on, among others, Brody Saxon,
   who was having an anxiety-induced asthma attack.
   He had turned white and was breathing
in big whooping gasps that took every ounce
   of effort he could muster. In his condition,

   Brody couldn't have faced a class of antsy kindergartners,
   much less the Viet Cong, but the doctors
kept passing him on from one test station to another
   because he didn't have any documentation
   which said he was sick, even though, by that point,
   he could barely stand. After the doctors
had finished with us, the sergeants herded us
   into a room filled with desks where we were to be given

the I.Q. test. First we had to fill in the information
on the front cover—name, address, and so on—
and then the sergeant told us to add up
   our total years of schooling and write the number
   on the front of the test booklet and circle it.
I figured twelve years of public school, four
of college, and three of graduate school made nineteen,
   so I wrote a big "19" on the cover and circled it.

   The test consisted of questions like,
   If you want to look up the meaning of a word,
you would use (a) the Bible,
   (b) the *National Geographic,* (c) the dictionary, or
   (d) the M-16 instructional manual,
   but since the desks were all close together,
and the test booklet was in big print,
   it was easy to see what answers everybody else gave,

   and I noticed that the guy to my right,
   who was holding his pencil in his fist the way
you'd hold a screwdriver, had drawn a big X
   through choice (a). For fifteen minutes or so,
   the room was completely silent except for the sound
of Brody Saxon's labored breathing. Then a sergeant
who'd been patrolling the aisles stopped at my desk,
   closed my test booklet, tapped the big "19" I'd circled

   on the cover, and stage-whispered, Fix that.
   It's correct, I said. Can't be, he said. It is,
I insisted. Look, he said, nobody spends nineteen years
   in school, no matter how dumb they are. I began
   to count on my fingers for him: twelve of public school,
   four of college, etc. By now everyone was looking at us,
and finally the sergeant just walked off, though not before
giving me a look that said, I've got my eye on you, buddy.

When the tests were over, I had failed:
I was in great physical shape and was smart enough,
despite all that time I'd spent in school, but I had
   a documented history of asthma and was therefore too much
     of a liability for the United States Army. Brody Saxon
was certified eligible for induction, and the sergeants
detained the deaf, crazy hippy for more tests. Later,
     on the bus back to Baton Rouge, I would show Brody my file

and tell him what sections of the Selective Service Code
   he needed to cite in his defense; eventually he appealed
his induction and got out of it. I never did find out
   what happened to the hippy, though I have the feeling
     he was just the kind of guy the Army was looking for
and that he ended up on the front lines somewhere, shooting
and being shot at when he should have been home smoking a joint
     and listening to his Iron Butterfly and Big Brother albums.

As I left AFEES that afternoon, I walked down
   to Bourbon Street to get a beer and celebrate
while I waited for the bus to take us back
   to our parents and sweethearts
     who were waiting for us nervously in Baton Rouge.
I walked into a bar and asked for a Busch,
which I really liked in those days because it had
     a big snow-capped mountain on the label

which, if you looked at it while you drank,
   really added to the pleasure of drinking the cold beer.
The bartender put the bottle on the counter
   and said that'll be a dollar, but as I was reaching
     for my wallet, the music came on and this bored stripper
   huffed out onto the runway and began to gyrate lazily.
Whoops, that'll be four bucks, said the barkeep,
     and I just looked at him as though he was crazy and left.

The Money Changer

When I arrived in Bogotá,
the first thing I wanted to do was change money,
    but Bill said not to use the banks
because he knew a black-market money changer
        who'd give me a much better rate.
So we went up to the eighth floor of this building
    and buzzed a door with an import-export logo on it.
A secretary looked at us quizzically
        and then went in the back to find her boss.
The front office was a dusty room with a bare desk in it
    and a cabinet that had a couple of curios on one shelf
to represent whatever it was that was supposed to be
        imported or exported. The boss came in all smiles
and handshakes and gave me one and a half times
    the official rate for my travelers cheques,
and he and I and Bill made a date to go out
        to dinner together the following week.

        Meanwhile, Bill and I were going camping
on the coast with some friends of his,
    so we bought provisions and packed our bags
and hired a driver to take us to Buenaventura,
        which was a sort of rough port town
from which we'd catch a boat to the campsite.
    There were six of us, three men and three women,
and we spent the night
        at a huge white colonial-style hotel
which prompted a lot of joking
    about how we expected Humphrey Bogart
to walk in at any minute
        and get us involved in some kind of dangerous
yet thrilling enterprise, like gun-running
    to the beleaguered rebels who either were
or were not in the vicinity, depending
        on which newspaper you read.

The next morning Bill and I went down
to check on boat times and saw some enormous black guys
   with shirt-splitting muscles jabbering away in Spanish
as they tossed around these fifty-gallon drums
           of molasses or cooking oil or cocaine extract as though
they were cans of soup. After a while,
   we felt sort of small and white,
so we went back to the hotel, where one of the women
           said that she had epilepsy
and had brought her Dilantin but forgot the syringe,
   and did we think it would be okay
if she just broke open an ampule and swallowed the stuff?
           Bill, who'd had medical training, gave her
a dirty look and went out to see what he could find
   in this little town that didn't have a pharmacy,
much less a doctor, though he finally did get a syringe,
           I think maybe from a veterinarian.

           The sea was really rough,
and when we got to the campsite,
   the crew put one end of this skinny plank
on the dock and then motioned for us to run down it;
           we had to wait for the boat to heel all the way over
in one direction and then jump on the plank
   and run onto the dock as quickly as possible
before the boat started heeling back the other way.
           Once we got the camp set up,
we all went down to the beach for a swim.
   The women took their tops off, but when they shouted
for the men to remove their suits, we wouldn't,
           because while we could see that the breasts of the women
looked all pretty and perky and pointy,
   once the cold Pacific waters struck our privates,
the result would be what's sometimes known as
           the old olive-in-a-bird-nest effect.

Now all this was pretty exciting to me,
because although all I had ever wanted to do,
   ever since I was a boy and my mother urged me to
become a photographer for the *National Geographic*,
            was travel and have adventures and then come home
to some big cosmoplitan city like New York
   while I waited for my next assignment.
But I'd lived in dinky places my whole life,
            and for the last ten years I'd been stuck
in the same little town; nothing had happened there
   except a divorce which was about as dramatic
and interesting as the marriage
            that preceded it. I mean, I had a job,
but that wasn't really going anywhere,
   and it was getting kind of difficult
for me to tell the difference
            between one year and the next.

            Within three days, all six of us had intestinal parasites,
and so we decided to go back. As we left Buenaventura,
   we were stopped by a platoon of soldiers
with automatic weapons who searched our van
            for forty-five minutes before letting us go.
We were so happy when we got back to Bogotá
   that we drank too much aguardiente
and had terrible hangovers the next day.
            The woman with epilepsy
said she'd been to my little town
   only once in her life, and that was late at night,
when she and a boyfriend had stopped at the Western Sizzlin'
            on Tennessee Street, where they were the only customers,
and as they ate their steaks, one of the bored waitresses
   looked at the boyfriend and said to her equally-bored
colleague, in a loud and uncaring voice,
            "Boy, I sure would like to fuck him."

Then the third guy in the group
said that *he* had been to Tallahassee only once
  and was in his car looking for a friend who lived on one
of the little streets near the FAMU campus when he saw a man
        aiming a shotgun at something across the road;
the guy figured that when he pulled abreast of the man
  with the gun, he'd lower it and let the car pass,
but the man with the gun just stood there,
        like a patriotic statue, until the guy driving
slammed on his brakes; by now the shotgun
  was sticking out across the hood of the car.
The man pulled the trigger; there was a bang and a flash
        and a loud "whark!" from the yard across the way,
and the guy in the car looked over in time
  to see this mutt flip through the air and fall lifeless
to the ground; evidently the man with the gun
        had just killed the bad dog of the neigborhood.

        The next night Bill and I and two of the women
went out with the money changer and his wife,
  and as we ate and drank rum and talked,
it gradually became apparent that the money changer
        had handled a lot of cash for some of the top people
in the narcotics business throughout South, Central,
  and North America, including a good many
who were connected with the CIA and other U. S. agencies,
        and as he talked, I felt the way I had
as Bill and I had watched the muscular black guys
  juggling those huge barrels back in Buenaventura.
The money changer seemed to be under a lot of stress;
        his manners were impeccable, but he talked loudly
and laughed just a little too much. On the other hand,
  I could see that he was really excited by his work
and got a lot of pleasure out of it,
        not to mention a great deal of nontaxable income.

During a lull in the conversation,
the money changer turned to me
  and lowered his voice and said,
with the precise enunciation of someone who knows
      a second language fluently but doesn't use it every day,
"Tell me, David, exactly what is it that you do?"
  For a moment I thought I'd say something like,
You know how you look out an airplane window
      and you see that the wing has hundreds
of these little screws in it?
  Well, I'm the one who patented that screw design,
so these days I just more or less collect my royalties
      and jet from spa to spa. Either that
or I'd been drafted by the Celtics
  but had blown out a knee in my third game
and had collected this huge settlement,
      so these days I just more or less, etc.

      By now, everyone at the table was looking at me,
so I said, "What was that again?"
  and he repeated his question, and I tapped my chest
and said, "You mean me?" and he said, "Yes, yes!
      What is it that you do?" So I took a breath
and tried to sound as though I didn't care
  and said, "Oh, I'm a university professor
in a small town in North Florida." The money changer
      dropped his knife and fork and pressed his hands
together on his chest; for a moment I thought
  he was having a heart attack, but then he said,
and I could tell from his tone that he was
      absolutely sincere about it, "To be a university
professor in a small town in North Florida—
  that must be paradise!" and I thought,
well, yeah, if you think about it,
      everybody's life is pretty interesting.

IV

It's big-leg music. It's generous and ample and hip shaking. It doesn't exclude anybody.

—singer/songwriter John Hiatt

The Talking Cure of Frau Emmy von N.

Her animal phobias apparently arose from her brothers and sisters
throwing dead animals at her at the age of five.
                        — Jonathan Winson, *Brian and Psyche*

It did not work.
She certainly could talk, though,
and had unusual strength of recall
and loved to reminisce,
so that Freud,
who was sitting there reflecting on his failure,
got the idea for free association,
though he didn't realize it until later.

So Frau Emmy did her part,
as did her brothers and sisters
and even the unknowing animals
who were weaseling around one minute,
emitting hippocampal theta rhythms like crazy,
the next lying there with all four paws
sticking up in the air
and their little tongues hanging out,
then being hurled
at the screaming Fräulein Emmy,

real heroes, every one: not like Tannhäuser,
who goes from ecstasy to remorse so quickly
that no one in the audience has believed it, ever,
or the prince in the story of Snow White
who promises to treat the dwarves
as his brothers and then abandons them,
forever ugly, forever alone in the woods.

Krafft-Ebing's *Aberrations of Sexual Life*

About sexual pathology he was never wrong,
the Old Master. How could he have been,
with everything there: the nun who could not
stop thinking about the morsel of flesh
lost at the first circumcision;
Holy Catherine of Genoa, who suffered so
from an inner heat so fiery
that she had to sit on the dumb earth
to cool down; the Heroines of the Whip
who cried, "This is not the death
I want to die, it is too filled
with pleasures and delights!"

He said you need three things to be
a doctor, the Old Master: knowledge,
experience, and goodness of heart.
But his subjects had no hearts—
their crimes were all so small.
How paltry they were, how stingy,
the shiteaters, the lovers of limping women.
Their enthusiasms are comic at first
and then sad, the best of them rarely, if oddly,
valorous, as in the soldier who wanted
nothing more than to examine his sweetheart's
sooty hands in the safety of a mirror.

Persons of Low Affect

All over the city
people are frozen
as in a painting by Di Chirico—
Melancholy, say, or *The Disquieting Muses*—
though for different reasons,
some wishing merely not to give alarm
to those waiting to get cash
from the automatic teller,
others genuinely lost in the wistfulness
of the just-graduated who have realized
that each must travailler comme une bête,
as Claude Bernard said to a student
who asked how he might succeed
in Bernard's laboratory,
or work with the persistence of an animal
and the animal's disregard for results,
because, deprived of its bone or nut,
it will not dwell on the absence
of the thing lost
but set about finding another,
without resentment.
Yet these people are filled with resentment
and hear only the voice
of the Parthian queen
who poured molten gold
down the throat
of the Roman triumvir Crassus, saying
Now you have what you wanted.

Anatomy of an English Madrigal

which ends with a reference
(though an apposite one)
to the title of a novel
by Choderlos de Laclos,
the song itself being called
"I Attempt from Love's Sickness
to Fly in Vain," the singer
of which is, as he tells us,
the source of his own fever and pain.
Yet the more he sings,
the happier he becomes
about his unhappiness;
indeed, the singer is so transported
that he begins to throw in
little embellishments,
turning "fly," for example,
into something like "fla-ha-ha-
ha-hy" as he becomes more
and more engrossed in
the musical expression
of his pain and less concerned
with the pain's verities.

But there is a lesson
to be learned,
even during those moments
when a person undertakes
to deceive himself
and regardless of the manner in which
that person characterizes
or fails to characterize
the nature of the profit
he means to derive
from such an undertaking,

and the singer's strenuous tone
at times comes so close
to hysteria as to suggest
that, in the process
of embellishing his few
if heartfelt lyrics,
somehow he has managed to discover
that the world is divided
against him, yes,
but also he is divided
against himself.
He is so lonely!
Loneliness is the great trap,
surely, yet each liaison
is a *liaison dangereuse.*

Your Famous Story

The table has been cleared,
and the guests are sitting around the fire

with glasses of brandy and chartreuse
as you begin to tell your famous story:

how you and your wife were desperate
to go somewhere, anywhere, after the birth

of your first child and finally found
a service in the yellow pages, a church group

that would send a babysitter, a gentlewoman,
a grandmotherly type who came highly recommended,

someone who had raised children of her own.
You went to a movie and a coffeehouse

and when you got back, the sitter was
just as you had left her, calm and smiling,

assuring you that everything had been fine,
that your little girl was an angel,

and you laughed, saying that she must not have
changed the baby's diapers or she would have seen

it was a boy. The sitter looked at the wall
and said in a voice you had never heard before

that while the baby might have been a boy
when you left, he was certainly a girl now.

You dashed upstairs and tore off the baby's pajamas
but of course he was fine, and that evening

you told your story for the first time to the police
and then, next morning, the church group.

They hid nothing, said the sitter had a history
of threatening children with knives,

but they were told all that was in the past,
and now the good liberal churchwomen were trying

to rehabilitate her with lay counseling
and the offer of regular work.

There was a hearing, and you told your story again.
The babysitter went behind walls.

Your son grew up healthy and strong,
and now he dines out

on the story you are telling us now,
the night coming down around your house

like a hand that closes around the heart,
opens a little, never lets go.

Eine Götterdämmerung in Mudville

This time he'll do it, they think—
tear the cover off the ball
like the much-despised Blake
or at least, like Flynn,
get a single.

And then it's over.
Days pass, months, years.
They turn and look at each other
as though each
remembers something:

Vergil's *Eclogues*,
the paintings
of Poussin
and Watteau, Balzac's
Comédie Humaine. . . .

As though each has seen
the god lie down heavily
beneath the trees, breathless,
the flesh thick
on his still-beautiful body.

Hunka Hunka Amor Caliente

Almost everyone I know has a secret life.
In most cases "secret" means "sexual,"
also "mental."
The general feeling seems to be that
we are all corpses on vacation,
therefore why not have two lives
and twice as much fun
before you have to jump back into that box?

However, "mental" does not mean easy.
Prostitutes say,
with respect to their customers,
"Even the nice ones aren't nice."
Therefore you have to be nice
but smart as well,
which probably means
avoiding prostitutes,

most of whom have awful expressions
on their faces, as though
they want to jump back into that box immediately.
I am an Ecclesiastes 8:15 man myself,
wherein it says, "A man hath no better thing
under the sun, than to eat, and to drink,
and to be merry," otherwise he jumpeth into that box
feeling a certain chagrin
and not the chagrin d'amour, either.

Same authority, chapter 9, verse 4:
"A living dog is better than a dead lion."
Your dog is not nice, though.
Your dog is nasty.
Too, your dog has to jump back into that box
a lot sooner than we do;
hence, no secret life for it.

For the rest of us
it's be nice, be smart,
get mental,
then back into that box
and zoom,
off to the undiscovered country.

Teeny Boy Moreau

My mother would chop off the heads of chickens
when I was a boy, chickens I knew the names of,
and they would run at me headless,
as if to say, you should have helped!

But that was only once or twice a year:
both my parents had jobs in town
and shopped for chicken at Letsworth's IGA,
brought it home to stew or fricassee.

Mr. Moreau and his brood lived
on the other side of Perkins Road
and were chicken farmers all day, every day—
they got up in the morning and started killing.

There was no boy there my age,
but my brother played with Teeny Boy Moreau
for a whole year and then announced one day
that my mother had to find him a friend in town,

that he didn't want to play with Teeny Boy
anymore. My parents tried to get him to tell
what was wrong, but my brother would only say
that Teeny Boy was mean, and, once, that

he knew too much about death. Mr. Moreau himself
died around that time, and when my mother
asked Teeny Boy how his mom was taking it,
Teeny Boy said she didn't know whether to shit

or go blind. My brother had a whole string
of new playmates before long, cheerful, bloodless boys
who played all day and stayed for supper,
boys who thought of themselves

no more than they wondered what was in the dishes
my mother made them, the jambalayas and tetrazzinis
and once, after she joined the Gourmet Club,
a heavenly *poulet à la comtoise.*

A Poor Unhappy Wretched Sick
Miserable Little French Boy

A little motherless French schoolboy
is traveling across America with his father,
and when they get to Reno,
the dad asks the boy if he would mind
his bringing a woman to their room
and the boy, who has a bad cold
from all of the air conditioning in America,

says yes, he would mind,
that it would make him feel funny,
and when the father says,
what do you mean, feel funny,
the little wretch says
he doesn't know what he means
and crosses and uncrosses his skinny white legs

and blows his nose into a big French handkerchief.
I too have felt funny without knowing why,
as when my boss says,
Could you step into my office a moment,
I'd like to have a word with you,
and I want to say I'd rather not,
it would make me feel funny,
or when my wife tells me she wants to have
a serious talk with me this evening
after I get home from work,
and I want to say, Oh, darling, let's not talk!
I'd feel funny if we were to talk!
At times like this,
I am the boy with the bad haircut,

the one in the cheap blazer and short pants,
my books in a strap the priests will take

to my nervous matchstick legs
if I stumble over my *verbes irregulières*.
I am turning into
a poor unhappy wretched sick miserable little French boy,
and the world is my angry, faithless father.

The Physics of Heaven

Everyone will be there at once:
your husbands and boyfriends
in their relation to you

as the wife and sweetheart of each
but also in equivalent if not identical relationships
with their other wives and sweethearts:

Harry, Edward and Maurice will coexist peacefully
with themselves and with you
but also with Sheila, Nancy, Kim, and so on

and all at the same time. And you, you'll be all
your happy selves: a little girl, a big girl, a woman,
a baby, everything except dead. And the pets!

Here's Beowulf, who died under the wheels of a milk truck,
          running
and playing again! And Matilda, who chased you
around the porch when she had distemper,

wagging her tail now as she licks your hand.
And all the fish who died before you could give them names,
though you meant to. And both hamsters.

And your parents, but this time they love each other,
which is to say they love themselves, love you.
It doesn't make sense. But no one notices, so it makes sense.

The Physics of Hell

No one you want to be here, is—
but the boy you invited to your twelfth birthday,
the one who called you that morning

and said he had a cold, even though
everyone else had seen him the night before
at the football game, running and laughing,

he's here—you were the only one without a date
at your own party because he wasn't there,
but he's here, smirking, empty-handed.

And the others, all the guys you'd broken up with,
they're here, too, with all the other girls
they've shamed and maddened, quarreling,

the din unbearable. It's the worst of times
and the worst of times. The friends who bored you
and then broke with you because you weren't interesting

are here, and so are the pets you starved,
the ones you let run in the street,
whose tails you pinched in the doors of their cages.

And you, you act selfish, break hearts—
you do what everyone else does, because hell makes sense.
But no one notices, so it doesn't make sense.

Nosebleed, Gold Digger,
KGB, Henry James, Handshake

Here's the thing: you're coming out of the men's room
and you run into someone you work with and he says

Hi, how's it going and you say Fine, you?
and he says Great and you go to your office

and he goes to the men's room and then
you run into him again on your way back,

only this time you say nothing to him and vice versa.
Is that because you don't have to or because

you don't want to? Nothing has changed
in those few minutes, surely, but perhaps you should ask,

and he should, too, because what if he had a nosebleed
in the men's room and needs to hear you say

That's nothing, happens to me all the time
or Here's the number of a good doctor?

Or say you got the bad phone call from your wife
who says That's it, you creep, I'm out of here,

giving this colleague the chance to say
You can get her back, give her this big ring,

or I always thought she was a cheap gold digger,
better luck next time. We could check on

each other constantly, of course, but that
would lead to crazy stuff, calling up in the middle

of the night to see if the other person is sleeping
or walking in on someone else's big sexy interlude

and saying Whew, you're doing great, thank god.
So let this poem be my signal to each of you

that I am thinking of you all the time;
if you're reading this, I'm looking out for you,

kind of: if you visited Russia in the old days,
the KGB would assign you a "minder" so you wouldn't steal

any state secrets but also to help you
if you get lost, and frankly, I'd rather be lost.

Also, what secret could the state have
that could possibly interest any right-minded person?

Be kind, be kind, be kind, said Henry James,
but that was easy for him to say, since he spent

most of his life alone. Nameless colleague,
I salute you and set down herewith my best wishes

for a *bonne continuation:* I shake your hand!
And you hers, and she his, and so on.